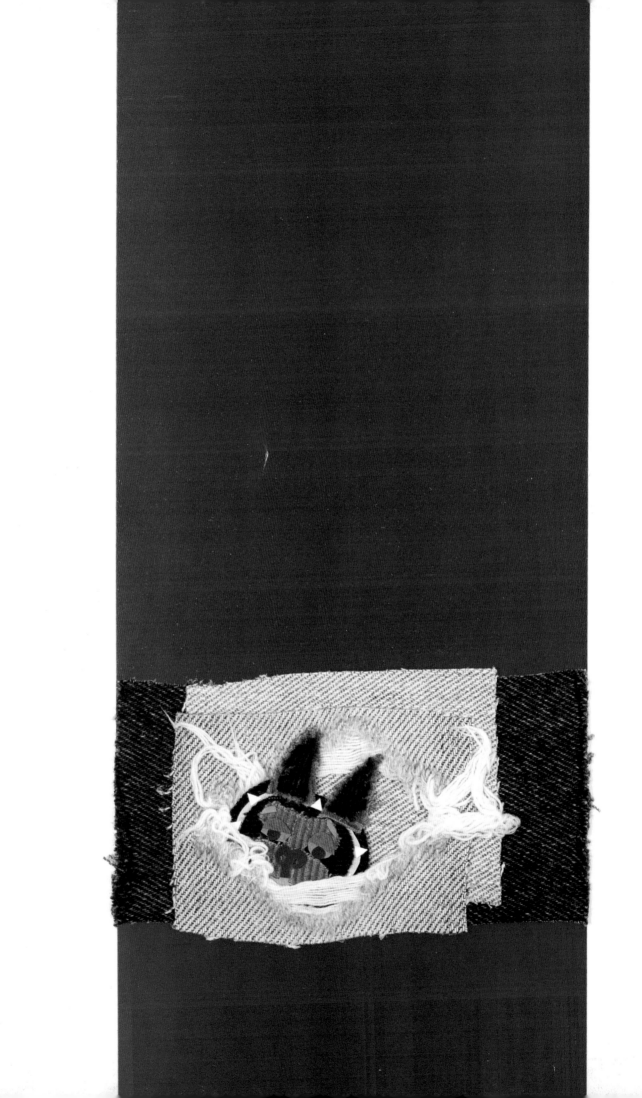

Debra Frasier

SPIKE

UGLIEST

DOG

in the

UNIVERSE

Beach Lane Books
New York London Toronto Sydney New Delhi

Thanks to my editor,
Allyn Johnston;
my husband and photographer,
Jim Henkel;
and the bounding dogs,
Harriett, Tesla, Dory, Tyler,
and Jim-the-Dog.

BEACH LANE BOOKS
An imprint of Simon & Schuster Children's Publishing Division
1230 Avenue of the Americas, New York, New York 10020
BEACH LANE BOOKS is a trademark of Simon & Schuster, Inc.
For information about special discounts for bulk purchases, please contact Simon & Schuster Special Sales at 1-866-506-1949
or business@simonandschuster.com.
The Simon & Schuster Speakers Bureau can bring authors to your live event. For more information or to book an event,
contact the Simon & Schuster Speakers Bureau at 1-866-248-3049 or visit our website at www.simonspeakers.com.
Book design by Lauren Rille
The text for this book is set in Calvert and News Gothic.
The illustrations for this book are collaged with Cansons papers, used clothing, and worn blue jean pieces. The jeans were gathered
from friends, students, coffee shop comrades, and thrift stores, as well as the author-illustrator's own collection. Bits and pieces of
paper, cloth, and denim were were adhered to cut-to-size Styrofoam garage door insulation with pins and repositionable glue, then
photographed with a Hasselblad 501C with a LEAF APTUS 65 digital back. The digital files were adjusted in Photoshop.
Manufactured in China
0713 SCP
First Edition
10 9 8 7 6 5 4 3 2 1
Library of Congress Cataloging-in-Publication Data
Frasier, Debra.
Spike : Ugliest Dog in the Universe / Debra Frasier.—1st ed.
p. cm.
Summary: Winning the Ugliest Dog in the Universe contest was awful for Spike, but when the cat Evangeline is threatened by a thief,
Spike proves that he is also good-hearted, loyal, smart, and much more.
ISBN 978-1-4424-1452-5 (hardcover) — ISBN 978-1-4424-8988-2 (ebook)
[1. Dogs—Fiction. 2. Pet adoption—Fiction. 3. Cats—Fiction.] I. Title.
PZ7.F8654Spi 2013
[E]—dc23
2012025585

For all our pets,
who help us to be better people

One day my owner entered me in the Ugliest Dog in the Universe contest.

I won.

It was awful.

New Times

#1

UGLIEST DOG: FOUND!

Thanks to his squat body, smashed-in face, droopy tongue, occasional drool, peculiarly pointed ears, stubby tail, and general all-around lack of beauty, it was unanimous: "SPIKE" is definitely the Ugliest Dog in the Universe. Spike trumped all other entered dogs to trot away with the blue ribbon.

These days there is little we can all agree on, but in this contest we finally found something!

VOTING CHANGES

My picture was on every porch in town—how embarrassing! But don't judge a book by its cover. A dog can't help the way he looks. Get to know me! I'm good-hearted. Loyal. Smart.

If you could see
    inside my heart,
        you'd say . . .

beautiful.

And then one morning my owner packed up his car and drove off.

"So long, Ugliest Pooch!"
he shouted.

I think he left me behind
because of his new girlfriend,
Sweetie. She only likes cats.
Big, fluffy, beautiful cats.

Did you say,

"How terrible"?

WAIT!

That night the boy from next door came over and untied me. His name is Joe. He fed me sausage scraps in a big red bowl, and he rubbed my head just the way I like it.

Humans can be very funny-looking, you know,
with those long, swinging arms and no fur
except on top of their heads,
but Joe—
he is

BEAUTIFUL.

He brought me to his house. I met his mom.
"Joe," she said, "I know you've always wanted a
dog, but we just can't afford one right now."
"Please?" he asked again.
"I'm sorry, sweetheart. This weekend we'll have
to take him to the animal shelter."

She meant the

DOG POUND!

But I belonged with Joe.

He belonged with me. We needed help!

So I turned to Evangeline.

She lives next door. She's won ribbons.

She's won trophies.

No one would ever abandon HER on the porch.

No one would ever take HER to the pound.

Desperate times require desperate measures.

And THAT included taking advice . . .

from a cat.

"Ohhhh yes," Evangeline
said, purring.
"I have the key—
you must simply be
more like me!

"No more useless tail wagging,
no more slobbering,
no more more digging,
no more chasing,
no more splashing,
no more muddy tracking.

Eat with care.

Stay clean. Stay quiet.

Stop this ridiculous barking!

Start all sounds with soft

PURRRRRRRRRRRRING.

And, ohhhh yes, never EVER miss a nap or skip a sardine snack."

Have you ever smelled a sardine?
Pew! Pew! PEWWWWWW!
It's a tiny fish with a **BIG** stink.

Evangeline licked her paws.
"Now it's time for my beauty sleep, ohhhh yes."

Desperate times
require desperate measures.

Agreed?

So I
tried.

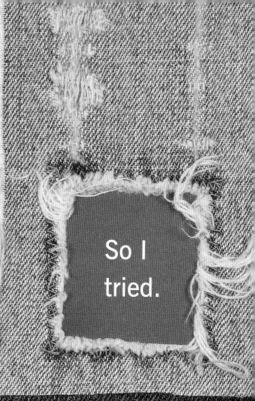

PURRRRRRRRRR
RRRRRRRRRRR
RRRRRRRRRR
RRRRRRRR
RRRRRRR

I didn't slobber. I didn't dig.
I was careful. Clean.
And most of all,
quiet.

Meanwhile, Joe started
a poster campaign.
He taped his drawings
all over the house.

Persuasive,
don't you think?

We made progress.

On Tuesday, Joe's
mom fed me her dinner
scraps. I ate them
slowly, with great care
and cleanliness.

On Thursday, more progress!

Joe's mom said, "Spike is so well-behaved. But strangely quiet, don't you think?"

"Such a sweet dog," she said on Saturday.

I was **CERTAIN** our plan was working.

But that afternoon when Joe lifted me into the truck, I wasn't so certain anymore. Things were TOO quiet.

We stopped at the hardware store.
I purred.
We stopped at the meat market.
I pretended to nap.
We stopped at the park.
I kept my paws clean.

Then it happened.

We turned in to—

the **DOG POUND!**

But guess what?

It was closed!

"We'll have to come back tomorrow," Joe's mom said.

Tomorrow? On the ride home, my heart broke.

Back at our house, Joe had homework to do. I curled up on the porch and went to sleep. Even Evangeline would have agreed with THAT plan.

I woke up to a familiar stink.
Pew. Pew. Pewwwwww.
I looked over the railing.
A trail of sardines on
the sidewalk?
Evangeline! Please.
Enough misery!
Not THAT smell.
Not NOW.

But wait—something was not right. I looked again.
It was a trick!

EVANGELINE!

Don't follow that sardine trail!

EVANGELINE!

Don't go into that dark hedge!

EEEEEE-
VAN-
GE-
LIIIIIIIIINE!

But I was too late.
The trap snapped shut.
A tall woman in sunglasses
snatched it up.

Ruff! Ruff! RUFF!

After her!

Nip! Nip! Bark! Bark!

I circled. I growled.
I grabbed her purse.
Her wig flew off!
She dropped the trap!
Evangeline yowled!

A car roared to the curb.
"Get in, Sweetie," the driver
shouted, "and forget about
that cat!"

Wait!

I knew that voice!

Tires squealed—
and the car was gone.
I ran to Evangeline.

"SPIKE!"

yelled Joe from the porch.

And suddenly neighbors were everywhere, cheering and clapping and carrying Evangeline around the yard.

The police came and asked questions.

Later the newspaper photographer arrived, but I wasn't about to go through THAT again. So Joe gave the reporter one of his drawings of me instead.

I watched it all from under the porch.
What was I thinking about?

Tomorrow, of course.

DOG POUND DAY.

And sure enough, tomorrow came.

"Come look! Spike is in the newspaper," Joe's mom called from the kitchen.

I covered my eyes. Oh, no. Not again.

"Spike," she read, "winner of the Ugliest Dog in the Universe contest, is a neighborhood hero! His lively barking saved the award-winning cat, Evangeline, from a thief. Spike's picture was drawn by Joe"—and her voice slowed— "the dog's new owner."

She looked up sharply. "Joseph, did you say that? Put Spike outside and come in here right now."

They talked for a long time.

And then we drove right
back to the dog pound.

WAIT! Hold your tears!
Did you know you can ADOPT a dog
at the dog pound?
Did you know they sell DOG LICENSES, too?
Did you know the reporter PAID Joe to use his
drawing in the newspaper?
AND they hired him to make drawings at the
next town dog show!

"Hey, isn't that the Ugliest Dog
in the Universe?" asked the
dog pound clerk.
"Don't judge a book by its
cover," Joe and his mom
answered together.
And then Joe's mom said the
most amazing words I've ever
heard.

Adoption Form
Name:
Add
Pet Nam

"Actually, he's the Most Beloved Dog in the Universe—and this is just the boy to take care of him."

She rubbed Joe's head just the way he likes it.

Now I have my very own tag.

Joe paid for it with money he made from drawing ME.

Isn't THAT **BEAUTIFUL?**

SPIKE
811 Sunny St.

Are you worried about Evangeline?
Don't be. She's home. Perfectly fine.

But she wants to be ready in case
there's more trouble ahead. So she
came to ME for help!

"Spike," she asked just this morning,
"could you teach me how to growl?"

"Ohhhh yes," I said.
"Right after our naps!"

WAIT! Don't go yet!
Look at Joe's report. . . .

SPIKE
811 Sunny St.

How I Draw Dogs
by
Joe K.

Instructional Essay
Mrs. Doppler – 5th Grade

Spike

How I Draw Dogs

Lots of people think drawing a dog is hard, but if you use my "Try, Try, Try" method you might find it easy!

You will need these art supplies: white paper, a sharp pencil and a black marker. Next, find a picture of a dog. In fact, find two or three in case you want to start over with a different one. (Some dogs are harder to draw.) For me it is easier to see the shapes in a photograph.

Start by looking at the dog's head. Trace the dog's photo with your finger. (I think my finger helps me to see.) The head is often shaped like a triangle with curves. (Except for my dog, Spike. His head is more like a watermelon.) Next trace the nose and eyes with your finger.

Now start on paper. Draw with a pencil first. (Draw sort of BIG, not tiny.) DO NOT WORRY ABOUT MESSY LINES!! Here is my secret: I draw a line over and over. I don't erase a bad line. This is the "Try, Try, Try" part. Eventually I pick the best line and make it darker. At the end I go over the best pencil line with a black marker.

    You can make your dog very simple, like these. Just add the body and legs to the head, drawing without many curves.

    In these next examples I added more curves. You can see my "Try, Try, Try" lines and the black marker tracing the best lines.

Now take your drawing to a bright window. Hold or tape another sheet of plain white paper over it. Trace the black line, skipping the "Try, Try, Try" lines. Presto! You drew a dog!